AN UNDERGROUND PRISON

Suddenly the truck plunged straight downward and stopped. They could hear the two men get out and slam the doors but couldn't see anything. It was silent for a few minutes and then they heard Ripper yelling.

"Hurry and get it covered up. It'll be daylight soon and we don't want no nosy neighbors seeing anything."

Something loud crashed over their heads, and they could hear dirt and bits of gravel hitting the top of the truck. It happened again and again. The last sound they heard was the scrape of a shovel picking up more dirt. Then it was quiet.

"I don't like it," Mitch said. "Something's wrong. Real wrong."

Roman moved to the windows. Nothing was visible. He tried the door. It was locked.

"Where do you think we are?" Woody asked. "It's really getting cold in here."

Roman hit the back door with his fist. "I'll tell you where we are. We're buried alive!"

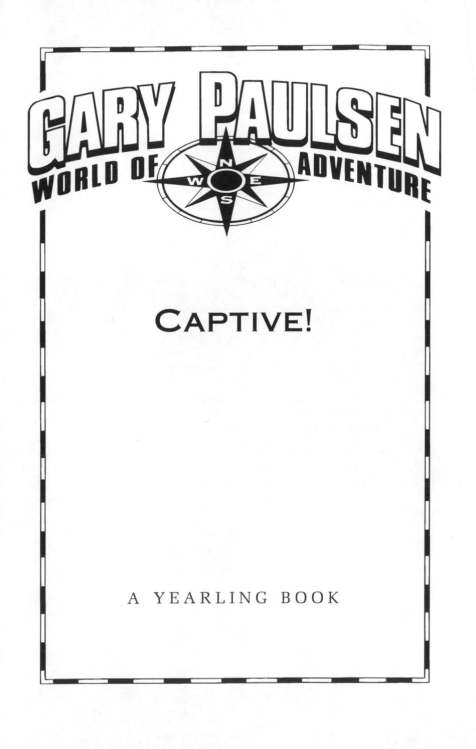

GARY PAULSEN
WORLD OF ADVENTURE

Captive!

A YEARLING BOOK

Published by
Dell Yearling
an imprint of
Random House Children's Books
a division of Random House, Inc
1540 Broadway
New York, New York 10036

ISBN: 0-375-89510-8

Series design: Barbara Berger

Interior illustration by Michael David Biegel

Printed in the United States of America

December 1995

Dear Readers:

Real adventure is many things—it's danger and daring and sometimes even a struggle for life or death. From competing in the Iditarod dogsled race across Alaska to sailing the Pacific Ocean, I've experienced some of this adventure myself. I try to capture this spirit in my stories, and each time I sit down to write, that challenge is a bit of an adventure in itself.

You're all a part of this adventure as well. Over the years I've had the privilege of talking with many of you in schools, and this book is the result of hearing firsthand what you want to read about most—power-packed action and excitement.

You asked for it—so hang on tight while we jump into another thrilling story in my World of Adventure.

Gary Paulsen

CAPTIVE!

CHAPTER 1

Roman Sanchez sat in the back of the classroom pretending to be asleep the way he always did. The bell had rung over ten minutes ago and the teacher was late. A paper airplane shot past Roman's head, just clipping his ear. He slowly opened one eye and looked up.

Woody—"the Worm"—Winslow was reaching cautiously for the plane when he noticed Roman stirring. He turned to run, but it was too late. Roman already had him by the back of his coat.

"Stuff the Worm in the trash can!" Jeff Dodsen yelled. Jeff was the captain of the Mason City Mustangs football team and the most popular kid in school. He started clapping and the whole class took up the chant.

"Stuff him. Stuff him. . . ."

Woody closed his eyes and waited for sure death.

It didn't happen.

Roman simply hauled Woody across the floor to his desk and dropped him like a puppy on the seat. Then the tall, quiet, dark-haired boy returned to his own desk, slid in, leaned back, pulled his cap low, and tried his best to get comfortable again.

The door opened and Miss Bently rushed in, carrying an armload of papers that smelled like fresh ditto fluid. She adjusted her glasses and looked disapprovingly at the paper wads and airplanes lying on the floor.

She cleared her throat. "Sorry to be late, class. Mr. Smathers was running off his se-mester tests, too, and as you know there's only one ditto machine, so I had to wait my turn."

Mitch Tyson, the president of the student

council, grinned up at her. "So does this mean we don't have to take the test now? Because we all know you wouldn't want us to be short on time and rush through it."

Miss Bently began passing out the test papers. "Nice try, Mitch. But no cigar. We still have plenty of time."

Silently the door behind her opened and closed. Two men wearing ski masks and dark clothes entered.

Someone in the front row screamed.

Miss Bently turned. The men were pointing guns at her and the class. She clutched the papers to her chest and backed up to her desk. "Wha . . . What is the meaning of this?"

The shorter man moved menacingly toward her, still pointing the gun. "School's out, Teacher. Have the kiddies all line up. We're going on a little field trip."

Miss Bently hesitated. The man slammed her against the desk, knocking the test papers from her hands. "I'm not playing games here, Teach. If you don't want nobody hurt you better line 'em up. *Now!*"

Frantically Miss Bently motioned for the

students to move away from their desks. They scrambled to obey, spilling books to the floor on their way.

The larger of the two gunmen, an enormous man with long, curly black hair pulled back in a ponytail, opened the door a crack and looked out into the hall. "It's clear, Ripper. Let's go."

The short man walked up and down in front of the kids, swinging his gun carelessly. "Listen up, students. We're all going to follow Spoon here, right down this hall and out the double doors. If you want to live, don't get out of line and don't make any noise. There's a school bus parked right outside the door—everybody gets on."

Chapter 2

 Anyone watching Miss Bently's class walk down the hall and across the school parking lot would have marveled at their seemingly perfect behavior. Not one student stepped out of the single-file line, and no one made a sound.

A closer look would have revealed the fear and confusion etched on their faces. One girl stumbled and fell to her knees. She was hastily helped to her feet by the student behind her so that there was no visible delay and their captors would have no reason to notice them.

Miss Bently's face had lost all color as she moved along behind her students. She felt somehow responsible for what was happening, but her mind refused to believe that any of this was real.

Inside the bus the two men pulled off their masks. The big man with the ponytail, the one called Spoon, slid into the driver's seat, closed the door, and cautiously pulled out of the parking lot onto the street.

The short man moved up and down the aisle, silently watching the kids. He was younger than the other man, blond and muscular. His mean, lizardlike eyes constantly searched the faces of the cowering students. His gaze lingered warily for a moment on a big kid with dark hair in the back of the bus who seemed to be sleeping. Then the man moved on.

The driver coughed nervously and checked the mirror every few seconds to see if they were being followed.

The bus had been outside the city limits for almost an hour, heading northwest. It was still quiet. The men barely spoke to each other, and only an occasional tense whisper could be heard from the back of the bus.

The short blond man continued to pace back and forth. Miss Bently had recovered enough to speak quietly to him when he reached the front. "Why are you doing this? These children all have families and homes. They'll be missed."

"That's what we're counting on, Teach."

"But the authorities will come after you. You can't hope to get away with this."

The man smiled and pulled something out of his pocket—a hand grenade. Miss Bently's hand flew to her mouth. She drew a sharp breath, and there was a scream from somewhere in the back of the bus. All eyes were on the grenade.

Ripper savored the moment. "Somehow I don't think they'll bother us. We left word that if any cops try to come near us, we'll blow this bus to kingdom come." He tossed the grenade in the air a couple of times and then slid it into his pocket. "You see, lady, you and your class are our hostages. You're our special insurance to make sure my partner and me get what we want."

"And what is that?"

"Don't talk to the dress, Ripper." Spoon glanced up into the mirror. "She don't need to know nothin'."

The blond man glared at him. "Shut up, Spoon. I'm running things and I'll decide who I want to talk to."

Spoon glared back but didn't say anything. He waved one hand in disgust and then concentrated on his driving.

Ripper turned his attention back to Miss Bently. "This is how it's going to work, Teach. I'm takin' you and your class to a special place out in the desert. It's so far out in the boondocks nobody could ever find us. After we get you settled, we'll let the cops in on the rest of our plan."

"Which is?" Miss Bently asked stiffly.

Ripper laughed a low, deep, satisfied laugh. "Simple. They bring us three million dollars and an airplane, and we give them back their precious little kiddies."

"What if they don't?"

Ripper grabbed the teacher's face and squeezed hard. "Then they don't get any of you back—ever."

CHAPTER 3

 The bus gave a lunge and jerked to a stop on the side of the road. Black smoke boiled out from under the hood, and the air smelled like burning rubber. Spoon cursed, threw open the doors, and rushed outside to see what the problem was.

He raised the hood and more thick black smoke came rolling out. Then he raced back inside and whispered something in Ripper's ear. Ripper quickly followed him down the steps.

"Now's our chance." Jeff Dodsen stood up and moved to the back exit of the bus.

Roman had been propped lazily in the corner of his seat as if the whole thing held absolutely no interest for him, but when he saw Jeff reach for the door he grabbed his arm.

Jeff jerked his arm away. "Hey! What are you doing, man? I think I can make it."

Roman whispered, "The door has an alarm, stupid. You wouldn't get ten feet."

Jeff's face flushed bright red. He sank into the seat across from Roman's, almost squashing Woody the Worm. "Then what do you suggest, hotshot? Just sit here and let that idiot blow us all to bits?"

Mitch Tyson held a finger to his lips. Then he let his window down so that he could hear the conversation going on outside. "Check it out, guys," he said in a low voice. "Those two are acting like they're real bus drivers and trying to get cars to stop and help."

"Look." Woody pointed out the window. "That delivery truck is pulling over."

A man dressed in a crisp white uniform stepped out of the truck and walked back to the bus. They saw Ripper give the man a toothy grin, shake hands, and lead him off to the side.

Spoon hastily squeezed through the bus doors and climbed the steps. "All right, everybody, there's been a slight change in plans. I know you'll be disappointed, but it turns out that some of you don't get to go on our little field trip after all." He moved down the aisle, looking at the students. "You." He pointed at Mitch. "Get outside. And you three in the back of the bus. Get off."

Roman put his head back and closed his eyes. He let out a deep breath, stood up, and started down the aisle after Mitch.

Jeff grabbed Woody and pushed the smaller boy ahead of him. He whispered loudly enough that Roman could hear him. "Look at the big man. Everybody at school thinks you're so tough. You're nothing but a big wimp—a yellow coward."

At the front of the bus, Miss Bently gave them a feeble smile. "Try not to worry, boys. I'm sure the authorities are doing all they can." She had tears in her eyes as the four boys moved down the steps and off the bus.

Outside they saw the delivery man lying facedown in the dirt beside the front wheel of the bus. Blood trickled from an open wound on the back of his head.

Ripper growled at his partner. "Get these kids in the truck, Spoon, and make it quick. We're behind schedule."

Spoon jerked open the back door of the delivery truck and motioned with his gun for the four boys to get in. He locked the door and headed for the driver's side.

Roman pulled his jacket around him and sat on the cold metal floor of the panel truck. The other boys crowded near the back and watched out the small round windows as they pulled away and the school bus disappeared from sight.

Chapter 4

 It was late at night, and in the back of the truck it was hard to see. Just about the time their eyes adjusted to the darkness, they would pass through another small town and the glare of the streetlights would flood in through the circular windows in the back door.

Mitch had discovered two loaves of bread that the delivery man must have forgotten, or hadn't had time to deliver, and passed them out.

Woody felt around in his backpack and found an apple left over from lunch. "Anybody want some? I don't have anything to cut it with, but . . ."

Roman pulled a knife out of his pocket. "Here, use this."

Woody fumbled with the knife and managed to slice the apple into four parts. He passed them out and handed the knife back to Roman. "What do you think those guys are going to do to us?"

Roman put the knife in his pocket. "For now . . . nothing. They need us alive."

"They obviously don't intend to feed us." Mitch bit into his piece of apple.

"I could have been long gone by now," Jeff muttered. "Next time—"

"Next time we'll wait for the right opportunity. Not some stupid move that'll get us all killed." Roman settled back against the wall.

"Who died and put you in charge?" Jeff smirked.

Roman sat up straight, dwarfing the other three boys. "Look, we've all got something to contribute here. Take Mitch. He's so full of bull, he could talk a bum out of his last dime. And the Worm's got enough brains to make an atomic bomb. And if we're real lucky, we might even find a use for you, Super Jock."

Jeff's jaw tightened and his fists doubled. "Oh yeah? All I know is you were the one who wimped out on the bus."

Roman leaned back again. "Save it, football brain. I'll be happy to settle the score when we get out of this."

The truck pulled to a stop, and the boys scrambled to the windows to see where they were. The truck was parked beside some old gas pumps at a small-town gas staion called Freddie's. An elderly man was on duty. He sat behind the counter, ignoring them, reading a newspaper.

Roman leaned close to Woody. "You got anything to write with in your backpack?"

Woody nodded and took out a green Magic Marker.

"Put it in your pocket. Mitch, the Worm and I need to get inside that gas station. See if you can convince them to let us out."

"Will do." Mitch knocked on the wall of the truck. The back door opened a crack and

Spoon snarled, "Keep it quiet in there or else."

Mitch whined, "We really, really gotta take a bathroom break, mister."

The door closed and then opened again. Spoon stuck his face in. "Ripper says okay. But only two at a time. Don't try anything funny or the two left out here won't last long."

Roman shoved Woody ahead of him. "You and I will go first."

Spoon followed them to the bathroom at the side of the station and waited for them outside the door.

Roman locked the door behind them. "Quick, give me the marker."

Woody handed it to him. "What are you going to do?"

"Watch." Roman went into one of the stalls and wrote on the wall:

Help. Tell the police—students being held hostage in white delivery truck were here at 2:00 A.M.

He wrote the date and paused. Woody touched his arm. "Why don't you put the license plate number? It's JXY 992."

Roman smiled. "I knew you were a genius."

Woody shook his head. "Photographic memory."

Spoon banged on the door. "Get out of there, you runts, before I blast the door open. Ripper's ready to go."

Woody moved to the door and unlocked it. Spoon pulled him out and pushed him toward the truck. "Tell the other two they're out of luck. Ripper won't wait no more."

When they were back inside, Woody looked at Roman. "Do you think it'll help much?"

Roman shrugged. "Depends. The police are probably trying to get a fix on our location. If somebody reports our message, they might get to us sooner."

"Big man," Jeff scoffed. "What would you know about the police?"

Mitch elbowed him. "His dad was a lieutenant on the force. He was killed in the line of duty last year. That's why Roman's a grade behind. He stayed home to help his mom."

"Shut up, mouth," Roman growled. "You talk too much."

"I heard your dad was part of a special forces SWAT team," Woody said. "Everybody says he taught you karate, and that the two of you used to go around the country giving exhibitions at schools and stuff."

The truck made a sharp left and pulled onto a gravel road.

"This may be something." Roman tried to listen. "From here on everybody pays attention. Nobody sleeps. I want to know every detail we can possibly remember from the time we left that pavement."

Chapter 5

 The truck was steadily climbing upward. They had turned right three times after leaving the pavement. Now they weren't even sure they were still on a road. The terrain was rocky and uneven, and they could hear tree limbs hitting the outside of the truck as it moved along.

"This doesn't make sense," Woody said. "Ripper told Miss Bently he was taking us to the desert."

"He lied, stupid." Jeff bounced in the air and came down hard. "Ouch! What do you think, he's gonna give away the location of his hideout so she can run and tell the police?"

"We could be anywhere." Mitch sighed and tried to find something to hold on to. "They'll never find us."

Suddenly the truck plunged downward and stopped. They could hear the two men get out and slam the doors but couldn't see anything. It was silent for a few minutes and then they heard Ripper yelling.

"Hurry and get it covered up. It'll be daylight soon and we don't want no nosy neighbors seeing anything."

Something loud crashed over their heads, and they could hear dirt and bits of gravel hitting the top of the truck. It happened again and again. The last sound they heard was the scrape of a shovel picking up more dirt. Then it was quiet.

"I don't like it," Mitch said. "Something's wrong. Real wrong."

Roman moved to the windows. Nothing was visible. He tried the door. It was locked.

"Where do you think we are?" Woody asked. "It's really getting cold in here."

Roman hit the back door with his fist. "I'll tell you where we are. We're buried alive!"

Chapter 6

 Jeff kicked the door. It didn't budge. He sat down in disgust. "What's the big plan now, smart guy? Thanks to you, we're all gonna die down here in this makeshift coffin."

"My dad always said when you're in trouble, take stock of everything you have." Roman took his knife out. "Let's take inventory. We've got my knife—"

"What good is a lousy knife going to do us?" Jeff sneered. "You think you're going to cut your way out of this metal can?"

"Shut up, Jeff!" Mitch yelled. "If you're not going to be part of the solution then just keep your mouth shut."

"I haven't heard a solution yet." Jeff folded his arms. "And anytime you think you're big enough to make me—"

"This isn't getting us anywhere." Woody sat on the floor near Roman. "The best I can figure, if the authorities go for Ripper's demands we'll be down here a couple of days. If they don't, then Ripper probably intends to leave us down here permanently. Either way he's not going to feed us or check on us."

Mitch rubbed his chin thoughtfully. "So what you're saying is, since they're not going to check on us we're free to do whatever we can to get out of here."

Woody nodded. "They probably dug this hole large enough for the school bus to fit in. So once we're out of the truck we'll have some room to move around."

Roman stood up and felt around one of the windows in the back of the truck. "If I can loosen this rubber seal maybe one of us could get through here."

Carefully he cut the seal with his knife. It was slow going because he couldn't see and had to feel his way around it.

"I think I've got it. Mitch, see if you can lift one of those bread racks down. We'll try to ram it through the window."

Mitch reached up and felt for the closest rack. "It comes loose. I think I can . . ."

Jeff moved over to help him. Mitch smiled in the darkness. "It's about time you learned to be a team player."

"Shut up and pick up your end."

When they got it down, Roman grabbed a side. "Woody, you get around on the other side. Okay, everybody back up a few steps. We'll run for the window on three. One . . . two . . . three . . ."

They made a wild charge. The heavy rack hit the little window and shattered it into a thousand pieces.

"Yes!" Woody shouted. "We did it."

Roman took off his coat and used it to clear away the sharp pieces of glass around the edges. "Come here, Worm. You're the smallest so you get to go through."

Roman lifted him up to the window. "Watch out for broken glass."

Woody crawled through headfirst and tumbled to the ground. He stood up and brushed himself off. "I'm out. Now what?"

"First let's have some light. I'm tired of being a mole."

Woody ran to the front seat and turned on the truck's inside light. The three boys in the back grinned at each other. Roman yelled, "Now the headlights!"

Woody put the headlights on and the underground cavern lit up. There was a space of about ten feet in front of the truck and only about two feet on either side. The roof of the hole was made of wooden planks covered with dirt.

Woody shook his head. "Man, if they'd driven the school bus in here it would have been a tight fit."

Mitch put his face in the window. "Say, Worm, how about letting us out?"

Woody found the keys Spoon had carelessly left in the ashtray and moved around to the back of the truck.

Jeff stepped out first. "Man, am I glad to be out of there. I honestly thought I'd never get out of this tin box."

Roman looked at his watch in the headlights. "It's gonna be daylight soon. If we want to get away from here, we better start moving."

He looked at the walls of the pit. They were all straight up and down except for the way they had driven in. Roman ran back to the driveway and climbed up the sloping dirt entrance. He pushed with all his might on the planks at the top, but they were too heavy for him to move.

"They must have piled a lot of dirt on top of us," Roman said. "We'll have to dig our way out. Look in the truck and get anything you can find to dig with."

In the glove compartment Woody found a screwdriver. Mitch pulled off the rearview mirror, and Jeff found a coffee mug under the front seat. Roman used Woody's screwdriver to loosen the license plate.

They climbed the slope and dug in a frenzy near the edge of the last plank. It was easy digging because the dirt was soft and already loose. It wasn't long until they had scooped out a small hole.

Roman nudged Woody and whispered, "Go back to the truck and turn off the lights. Grab your pack and anything else out of the front you think might be useful."

One at a time they inched out of the hole. Woody was the last one out. He handed up his pack and then climbed out after it.

It was too dark to tell anything about their location. Roman thought he could make out the shape of a house nearby, but he couldn't be sure. And for all they knew it could be the kidnappers' hideout.

"What I wouldn't give for a flashlight right about now," Roman whispered.

"No flashlight." Woody reached in his pack and brought out a small white package. "But I did find some matches."

"Great. Come on." Roman headed for some nearby trees. "Let's find some cover and decide what our next move is."

Chapter 7

 "We've been walking for hours." Mitch stopped to catch his breath. "The sun's up and we're going nowhere. I think I've seen these same stupid trees three times."

Roman sat down on a rock. "You're right. None of us knows anything about traveling in the mountains. If we're not careful, we'll wind up lost and in worse shape than we were before."

"I'm pretty sure we should keep heading downhill," Woody said. "I read somewhere that you should do that if you ever got lost."

"We've been heading downhill, Worm." Jeff fell to the ground beside Roman. "We just keep running into more trees."

Woody wiped his face with the back of his dirty hand. "All I know is we better keep moving, or those guys are going to find us."

"Shoot, they don't even know we're gone." Jeff put his hands behind his head and re-laxed against the trunk of a tree. "We went back and covered up the hole, remember? Those dummies think we're safe and sound buried underneath the ground."

"Did you hear that?" Woody strained to lis-ten. "It sounded like an engine."

Roman jumped up. "It's a car. And that means there's a road nearby. Come on."

They crashed through the trees and oak brush right on Roman's heels, racing toward the noise. In a few seconds they were standing at the edge of a dirt road.

"You did it, Worm!" Jeff shouted. "Now all we have to do is wait for that car to get here."

"Just to be on the safe side, I'll wait for the car," Roman said. "We wouldn't want to run into those creeps again. You guys stay in the bushes until I give you the signal."

Roman stood in the shadows next to a tree and watched the others scramble into the bushes. The car was coming closer, moving slowly. It was an older model, rust-colored, with four doors. Finally it rounded the corner and Roman could see the driver, a young woman with long black hair.

Roman stepped out from behind the tree and waved furiously for the driver to stop. She slammed on the brakes and rolled down her window.

"You gave me quite a start. I didn't expect to see anyone way out here."

Roman leaned down. "You've got to help us, ma'am. My friends and I were kidnapped. We escaped and now we have to get in touch with the police."

"I'd be glad to help you in any way I can." The woman looked around. "Did you say you were with friends?"

"Oh yeah." Roman motioned for the others to come out of the bushes. "We were afraid you might turn out to be the kidnappers, so they hid until we were sure."

The woman watched Mitch and Jeff crawl out of the oak brush. Woody hung back. She turned to Roman. "Why don't you and your friends get in, and I'll take you to my house. I live right up the road. You can call the police from there."

Roman opened the back door, and Mitch and Jeff climbed in. Woody grabbed Roman's sleeve. "I really need to talk to you."

"Not now, Worm. This lady's taking us to a phone. Get in."

"But Roman—"

"Get in, Worm. We don't have all day."

Woody sighed and climbed in beside Jeff. Roman went around and got in on the passenger side. "We sure appreciate this, ma'am. We were just about ready to give up on ever finding our way out of these mountains."

"I'm glad to help." The woman looked in her rearview mirror at the other boys. "You guys look like you could use a hot meal."

"Could we ever." A grin spread across Jeff's

face. "My stomach feels like my throat's been cut."

Roman looked back at Woody. The boy seemed nervous. "You okay, Worm? You don't look so good."

Woody slowly shook his head and pointed at the woman in front of him. Roman frowned. "I don't get it."

"Don't get what?" the woman asked.

"Oh, nothing." Roman glared at Woody. "My friend is still a little upset from what we just went through."

The woman pulled off on a side road. It was rough, and they bounced up and down on the seats.

Woody leaned close to Jeff and whispered, "Does this remind you of anything?"

"Yeah, it's kinda like the road we were on last—" He clapped his hand over his mouth and his eyes grew wide.

The woman pulled to a stop in front of a run-down wooden house. "Here we are, boys. Go right on in and make yourselves at home."

The screen door opened and two men with

guns stepped out on the porch. The short blond one walked around the car.

"Thanks, Madge. Good thing you were supposed to report in today or our little hostages might have gotten clean away."

CHAPTER 8

The woman stood on the porch, talking to the two men. They were laughing and pointing at the car.

Roman leaned over the back-seat. "If you knew she was one of them, why didn't you say so?"

"At first I didn't know." Woody looked miserably down at the floorboard. "There was just something about the car that seemed familiar. Then I remembered where I had seen it before. It was in the school parking lot the day we were kidnapped."

"What a bunch of chumps we are," Jeff said. "Of all the people in the world, we have to flag down their accomplice."

"What do we do now?" Mitch whispered.

"Doesn't look like they're planning on giving us much of a choice." Jeff pointed in front of them. Ripper and Spoon were coming toward the car.

"All right, you punks," Ripper growled. "Get out of there."

The boys reluctantly climbed out of the car, and Ripper pushed them toward the old house. "This time we're gonna make sure you runts ain't goin' nowhere." He followed them through the front door. "Everybody down on the floor. Find something to tie 'em up with, Spoon." Ripper picked up a ball of twine from the table and threw it at the large man. "Here, use this, and make it tight." He turned and went back out to the porch to talk to the woman.

Roman looked around the room. It was sparsely furnished. A rickety table and two chairs stood near the door, and there were a couple of army cots under an open window near the back wall. There was a shortwave radio on a wooden shelf above the table.

"You're the last one. Get your hands out, kid." Spoon knelt down in front of Roman. Roman stuck out his hands with his wrists crossed. It was the oldest trick in the book, but it was worth a try.

Spoon fell for it. He pulled the twine tight, then ran it down to Roman's feet, tied them together, and cut the end of the rope with a butcher knife.

Spoon stood up and grinned. "Now you boys just make yourselves comfortable, 'cause you're gonna be here awhile." The big man tossed what was left of the twine into the corner of the room and headed out the door.

"Man, these ropes are tight." Woody squirmed, trying to find relief. "I think they're cutting off my circulation."

Roman uncrossed his wrists and easily pulled his hands out of the cords. Quickly he reached into his pocket for his knife and cut the twine around his feet. He moved to

Woody and had started to cut him free when he heard someone coming.

"I'll be back," Roman whispered. He ran to the first cot, made a flying jump, and leaped out the open window headfirst. He hit the dirt in a tight little ball, scrambled to his feet, and ran as hard as he could for the bushes.

The door opened and the three kidnappers walked in, still talking and laughing.

The woman stopped when she saw the boys. "Wait a minute. One's missing."

"Spoon, you idiot! Can't I trust you with anything?" Ripper stormed across the room to the boys and slapped Woody hard, knocking him sideways. "Where did he go?"

Woody struggled to sit up. Blood was dripping from his nose. He set his jaw and glared at Ripper.

Ripper had drawn his hand back to strike again when Madge spoke up. "That big kid will be halfway to town if you and Spoon don't quit fooling around and go after him."

"She's right, Ripper—" Spoon started.

"Shut up, you moron. If it wasn't for you he

wouldn't he loooo." Ripper took his gun out of his belt and checked the clip. "Madge, you stay here and keep an eye on the rest of them." He pointed the gun at Spoon. "You better hope we find that kid."

CHAPTER 9

Roman burrowed his way into a thick section of oak brush and tried to lie as still as possible. His heart was pounding. He couldn't see anything but he could hear the two men yelling back and forth.

Then it was quiet. Spoon had found some tennis shoe tracks the boys had made the night before and was following them deeper and deeper into the woods. Ripper had taken the car and was checking the roads.

Roman sat up. His mind raced. They must have left the woman behind to watch the others. If he was going to try anything, it would have to be now, while the two men were gone.

He took a deep breath, inched out of the oak brush, and looked around. There was no sign of anyone. Quietly he made his way to the window, edged up to one corner, and peeked in. The woman was sitting at the table with her back to him, reading a newspaper. She was tapping the table over and over with her long red fingernails.

Carefully he moved toward the middle of the window until he caught Jeff's eye. Jeff nodded. Roman took the knife out of his pocket and tossed it lightly onto the end of the cot.

Roman moved back and watched Jeff working his way over to it. He had to scoot along the floor, trying not to attract any attention. Once he reached the cot, he had to reach up quickly to grab the knife before Madge turned and saw what he was trying to do.

She looked up just as he snatched it. "What are you doing over there?" She stood up and took a step toward him. "If you think you're going out that window, think again. Get away from there." She marched over to the window and slammed it shut as Roman ducked around the side of the building.

Jeff kept his fist tightly closed over the knife and moved back to Woody and Mitch.

The woman folded her arms and walked around the three boys. "You squirts better not be planning anything. It won't do you any good. I had a talk with Ripper earlier. I told him I thought there were too many of you. He wouldn't object to getting rid of one or two of you. All I have to do is give the word."

She gave them a long, disgusted look and then went back to the table to read her paper. But this time she turned her chair toward them and looked up every few seconds.

With as little movement as he could manage, Jeff opened the blade and sawed at the twine on his hands. It was difficult work since his hands were tied, but in minutes the twine snapped. He kept his hands close together and silently worked on his feet.

Roman heard the faint sound of a car engine

coming from somewhere down the road. He knew it wouldn't be long until Ripper was back. His choices were getting narrower.

He took a breath, centered himself, and ran to the front door, shoving it open. Madge stood up so fast her chair fell backward. She reached into her purse, pulled out a small gun, and pointed it at Roman.

"You get over there with your friends, kid, and I won't hurt you."

Jeff tossed the knife to Mitch and jumped to his feet.

Madge swung around. Jeff stepped closer. "What are you going to do, lady? You can't get both of us."

The woman slowly backed into the corner. "Stay away. I mean it. I'll shoot."

Roman waited for her to look over at Jeff again. The second she did, he jumped in and landed a swift karate kick, knocking the gun out of her hand. It sailed across the room and dropped through a hole in the old wooden planks to the dirt below. Madge slumped to the floor, holding her wrist.

"All right!" Jeff slapped hands with Roman.

Mitch had just finished cutting the last piece of twine on Woody's feet. Woody rubbed his ankles. "What took you so long?"

"Shut up, Worm." Mitch playfully punched him in the shoulder. "Your nose okay?"

Woody nodded and looked at Roman. "What do we do now?"

"Grab the radio. We've got to get out of here. I heard Ripper coming back. He could be here any second."

CHAPTER 10

 "In here." Roman led the way into a dark thicket. "We'll rest for a few minutes. We've been moving hard for the last couple of hours." He reached for the radio. "I don't know what good it'll do to call out, since we don't have a clue where we are."

Woody sat down and dumped the dirt and rocks out of his tennis shoes. "It couldn't hurt, and right now it's about the only hope we have."

Mitch was puffing like a bellows. He leaned over and put his hands on his knees, trying to catch his breath. "Man . . . I'm tired. What I wouldn't give . . . for a cool . . . glass of water."

Jeff fell to the ground and stretched out. "Somebody wake me when this nightmare is over."

"Don't get too comfortable." Roman set up the radio. "We're moving out again in a couple of seconds. Ripper and Spoon could be anywhere. They know the area. We don't."

He pressed the transmission button. "Hello, does anybody out there hear me? My name is Roman Sanchez. I was kidnapped along with three other guys two days ago." Roman let go of the button and listened.

Nothing.

He tried again. "If you can hear me, we need help. We have escaped from the kidnappers but they're after us. I'm not sure of our location. All I know is that we're on a mountain, somewhere near a small gas station called Freddie's." He listened again. There was no response.

Roman packed up the radio. "I'll try again later. We better be on our way."

"On our way to where?" Jeff asked. "It's getting late and we don't even know which direction to head."

"Like the Worm said, we should keep going downhill." Roman started walking. "This time I have a pretty good idea where the road is. I've been trying to stay out of sight and still keep it to the left of us."

Mitch moved up beside him. "Do you think there's any chance we'll make it to that little town we drove through before it gets too dark?"

Roman shrugged. "Who knows? All I know is the farther away from those guys we can get, the better."

They walked single file for the next mile without talking. The sun was almost down and it was starting to get cold.

Mitch broke the silence. "If we keep going in this darkness, somebody's gonna trip and break a leg or something. Maybe we should find someplace to lay up until daylight."

"He's right, Roman," Woody said. "I'm worn out. Those guys aren't going to find us in the dark. We can get a fresh start in the morning."

Roman hesitated. "I don't know . . ."

"Come on. It'll give you a chance to try the radio again." Jeff pointed to some trees. "We'll spend the night over there." He patted Roman on the back. "I'm not worried—if anything goes wrong, we've got the Karate Kid on our side."

CHAPTER 11

 Roman's eyes flew open. It was morning. He needed to get everybody up and moving. He stretched. His neck was stiff from sleeping on the cold ground. He was about to turn over on his makeshift bed of leaves when, out of the corner of his eye, he caught a flash of movement.

A sharp-toed cowboy boot was coming at him. He rolled but it still hooked him in the ribs. He groaned in agony and tried to stand up. The boot came at him again, this time catching him in the stomach and knocking the wind out of him. He rolled into a ball and looked up.

Ripper stood over him. "You thought you were pretty big stuff yesterday, didn't you, hero? What's wrong, kid? You don't seem so tough today." The blond man laughed and looked over at his partner. "Does he, Spoon?"

Spoon shook his head. He was standing behind Mitch, Woody, and Jeff with his gun out. "No. In fact he looks kinda sick today. Maybe he ain't feeling so good."

"Leave him alone." Woody took a step toward Ripper. "Pick on somebody your own size."

Ripper burst out laughing. "Like who, half-pint? You?"

Woody glared at him. "Leave us alone. We haven't done anything to you."

"Wrong again, little man." Ripper stepped in front of him. "You four have given me a lot more trouble than you're worth. But that's going to stop because we've decided to move you to a different place. A place where you'll never be heard from again."

The three boys glanced at each other,

"Get your friend up," Ripper ordered. "We're going back to the cabin."

Jeff and Mitch tried to help Roman to his feet. Halfway up, Roman drew a sharp breath and held his left side in pain. "I think a couple of my ribs are broken."

"Here. Put your arm around me." Jeff moved to the right and let Roman use him as a crutch.

"You shouldn't have kicked the kid so hard," Spoon said. "He's gonna be all day getting back to the cabin at this rate."

"What are you griping about? They're not supposed to deliver the money to the airstrip until tonight. By that time we'll have these little problems of ours safely tucked away and we'll be on our way to the good life in South America."

Spoon grinned and pushed Mitch and Woody ahead of him. "I think I'm gonna like being rich."

Woody stumbled forward. "You'll never get away with it. In the last century there hasn't been a single time when this type of crime was successful."

Spoon frowned. "What's he talking about, Ripper?"

"Nothing. He's just running off at the mouth."

Mitch looked back at Spoon. "I'd listen to him if I were you, mister. He's a walking encyclopedia. There isn't anything he doesn't know."

"See if he knows how to keep his mouth shut," Ripper growled. "That goes for the rest of you, too. No noise until we get back to the cabin."

Chapter 12

"Break's over. Get the big kid up. We're almost there." Ripper watched Jeff help Roman stand. "I wouldn't want to be in your shoes when Madge gets ahold of you. She'll probably tear your eyes out. She's pretty mad about what you did to her yesterday."

Roman struggled to his feet. He ignored Ripper and started walking. When they were a few feet away, he whispered to Jeff, "After we get there, I'll start something and you guys make a run for it. It may be your last chance."

"No. We're not leaving you."

"You have to. I—"

"No talking," Ripper barked. "Spoon, get the rest of them up here. The cabin is just over the next hill. I don't want to take any more chances."

Mitch walked up beside Jeff. "Want me to take over for a while?"

Jeff shook his head. "No, I'm doing okay."

They crossed the road and started down the bumpy path to the cabin. Woody studied the ground. His photographic memory immediately noticed something different. Quickly he moved to the other three and pretended to help Roman.

"New tire tracks," he whispered.

Roman looked around. "Be ready for anything."

When they topped the hill, the cabin looked the same as it had when they'd left. Madge's old car was still parked out front.

"Go tell her we're back," Ripper ordered. "I'll load the boys in the car."

Spoon went into the cabin, and Ripper

opened the back door of the car. "Get in, kiddies. This will be the last ride you'll ever take. Enjoy it."

Woody bent down to tie his shoe. Mitch stopped at the car door. "Listen, mister, we haven't had anything to drink in three days."

"My heart bleeds for you, kid. Get in the car." He yelled over his shoulder at the cabin. "What's takin' you two so long? Get out here!"

There was no answer.

Ripper's eyes narrowed. "Spoon?"

Silence.

The front door opened and a tall, well-dressed man stepped onto the porch. Several more men moved out of the brush around them.

The man on the porch flashed his badge. "Give it up, Ripper. We've got your partners. Drop your gun and move away from the boys. There's no way out."

Ripper acted as if he were going to drop his gun but then whirled and grabbed Mitch with one arm, using him as a shield.

"You cops come any closer and this kid won't see his next birthday."

"Give it up, Ripper. You can't win." The man on the porch edged down the steps.

"Don't come any closer!" Ripper screamed. "Everybody get back."

The agent near the porch put his hands up. "Don't do anything stupid."

Roman let his arm quietly slide off Jeff's shoulder. He held his side tightly and jumped. One foot jabbed into Ripper's stomach, making the blond man drop the gun and double over. Before anyone could blink, Roman brought the other foot up under Ripper's chin, spinning him around.

In seconds the agents had surrounded Ripper and handcuffed him.

"Way to go, Roman!" The boys crowded around him, slapping him on the back.

"Hey, watch the ribs . . ."

"Are you Roman Sanchez?" The agent who had done all the talking walked up to them and put out his hand. "I'm Sam Williams. I worked on a few cases with your father years ago. He'd have been proud of you today, son."

"Thanks." Roman stared at the ground, embarrassed.

"How'd you find us?" Woody asked.

"We had the general area pretty well pinpointed after we got your message at the gas station. But what helped at the end were your radio transmissions. You boys really used your heads."

Roman looked at the tired, dirty faces of the other three boys. "We had a lot of luck, all the luck there is."

"Luck, nothing!" Woody held both fists in the air. "We're just too awesome for 'em to hold, right, guys?"

Jeff moved to Roman and supported him while he sagged in pain, helping him to the porch. "Right, Wormy—totally awesome. At least one of us."

"You know what I think?" Roman said, wincing and watching the officers put the kidnappers in the backseats of government cars.

"What?" Jeff asked.

"I think next year we should do something else on our field trip."

GARY PAULSEN
ADVENTURE GUIDE

HIKING SURVIVAL GUIDE

The best rule of thumb in any situation is *be prepared.* This is especially true in hiking because the wilderness often makes special demands on those who use it.

Before you go, make sure you have the right gear and clothing, and that you are physically able to withstand the rigors of the trail. Make a checklist of the things you need to be sure that nothing will be left behind.

Gear for a one-day hike might include a map, a flashlight, a compass, matches, a small first aid kit, a rain poncho, a sweatshirt, a pocket knife, a whistle, a canteen, and lunch. All of this can be easily carried in a lightweight rucksack.

If you become lost, there are a few simple rules to follow. Keep calm and trust your map and compass. If you can't find your position, clear an area and build a signal fire. Don't get caught by darkness. Find a shelter and spend the night.

Planning ahead can make hiking a unique wilderness experience that anyone can enjoy.

GARY PAULSEN

Gary Paulsen has written many popular novels for young people, including the Newbery Honor books *Hatchet, Dogsong,* and *The Winter Room.* He is an avid outdoorsman who has twice raced in the Iditarod, a 1,180-mile dogsled race across Alaska. He has journeyed from New Mexico to Alaska by motorcycle, has sailed the Pacific Ocean, and frequently takes pack mule trips into the mountains. Gary Paulsen and his wife, the artist Ruth Wright Paulsen, have homes in New Mexico and on the Pacific.